by **Harriet Ziefert**

illustrated by **Ethan Long**

W9-DIB-739

YOU and Me: WE'RE OPPOSITES

Livonia Public Library
ALFRED NOBLE BRANCH
32901 PLYMOUTH ROAD
Livonia, Michigan 48150-1793
421-6600
LIVN #19

Blue Apple Books

I'm up.

You're down.

I'm big.

You're little.

I'm in.

You're out.

I sit.

You stand.

I'm tall.

You're short.

I have a lot.

You have none.

You're dirty.

I'm clean.